D1735718

Community Helpers

Pilots

by Erika S. Manley

Bullfrog Books

Ideas for Parents and Teachers

Bullfrog Books let children practice reading informational text at the earliest reading levels. Repetition, familiar words, and photo labels support early readers.

Before Reading

- Discuss the cover photo. What does it tell them?

- Look at the picture glossary together. Read and discuss the words.

Read the Book

- "Walk" through the book and look at the photos. Let the child ask questions. Point out the photo labels.

- Read the book to the child, or have him or her read independently.

After Reading

- Prompt the child to think more. Ask: Have you ever been on an airplane? Did you see the pilot?

Bullfrog Books are published by Jump!
5357 Penn Avenue South
Minneapolis, MN 55419
www.jumplibrary.com

Copyright © 2020 Jump! International copyright reserved in all countries. No part of this book may be reproduced in any form without written permission from the publisher.

Library of Congress Cataloging-in-Publication Data

Names: Manley, Erika S., author.
Title: Pilots / by Erika S. Manley.
Description: Minneapolis, MN: Bullfrog Books, Jump!, Inc., [2020]
Series: Community helpers
Includes bibliographical references and index.
Identifiers: LCCN 2018056976 (print)
LCCN 2018057627 (ebook)
ISBN 9781641288361 (ebook)
ISBN 9781641288347 (hardcover : alk. paper)
ISBN 9781641288354 (pbk.)
Subjects: LCSH: Airplanes—Piloting—Vocational guidance—Juvenile literature.
Air pilots—Juvenile literature.
Classification: LCC TL561 (ebook)
LCC TL561 .M276 2020 (print)
DDC 629.132/52—dc23
LC record available at https://lccn.loc.gov/2018056976

Editor: Jenna Trnka
Design: Shoreline Publishing Group

Photo Credits: wavebreakmedia/Shutterstock, cover; ESB Professional/Shutterstock, 1; Jelena Aloskina/Shutterstock, 3; MH Lee/Shutterstock, 4; Angelo Giampiccolo/Shutterstock, 5; IM–photo/Shutterstock, 6–7; Ambrozinio/Shutterstock, 8–9, 23br; Tunedin by Westend 61/Shutterstock, 10–11, 23tl, 23tr; Atosan/Shutterstock, 12–13, 23tm; Aleksandr Bognat/Dreamstime, 14 (hands); Mike Focus/Shutterstock, 14 (screen), 23bl; Ingo Wagner/picture-alliance/dpa/AP Images, 16–17; Philip Pilosian/Shutterstock, 18; Mike2focus/Dreamstime, 19; Olena Yakobchuk/Dreamstime, 20–21; Alexey Petrov/Dreamstime, 22; Nadezda Murnakova/Shutterstock, 23bm; BoonritP/Shutterstock, 24.

Printed in the United States of America at Corporate Graphics in North Mankato, Minnesota.

Table of Contents

Let's Fly!

Kara wants
to be a pilot.

What do they do?

They fly airplanes.
Cool!

wings

A pilot wears a uniform.
This includes a hat
and wings.

pilot

The pilot is in charge of the airplane.

She sits in the cockpit.

So does her copilot.

copilot

They run
the controls.

Oh, no!

There is a storm ahead.

Pilots look at the forecast.

They know to fly
around the storm.

seat belt sign

The pilot puts the seat belt sign on.

We stay in our seats.

The pilot helps keep us safe.

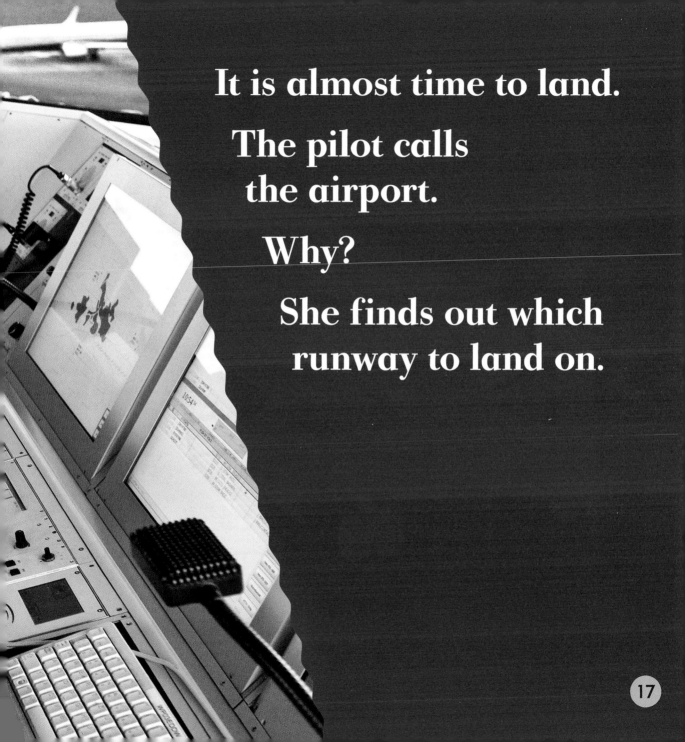

It is almost time to land.

The pilot calls
the airport.

Why?

She finds out which
runway to land on.

The pilot lowers the airplane's wheels.

wheels

It is a safe landing.
Nice job!

runway

19

Pilots fly us safely.
Thank you!

In the Cockpit

controls
There are many controls in the cockpit to help pilots and copilots fly and navigate the aircraft.

headset
Pilots have headsets and radio systems to talk to air traffic control and other pilots on their same flight paths.

Picture Glossary

cockpit
The control area, in the front of an airplane, from which it is piloted.

controls
The levers, switches, and other devices that make a machine work.

copilot
The assistant pilot of an airplane.

forecast
A prediction of what the weather will be like in a certain area.

runway
A strip of hard, level ground that aircraft use for taking off and landing.

uniform
A special set of clothes worn by a member of a group or organization.

Index

To Learn More

Finding more information is as easy as 1, 2, 3.

❶ Go to www.factsurfer.com

❷ Enter "pilots" into the search box.

❸ Choose your book to see a list of websites.